TURN ME ON

The Desire of a Flirtatious Woman

TOMLIN WAYNE

Chapter 1

Jeff was practically vibrating with excitement. Everything needed to be just so. He meticulously reviewed the setup of the desk, its precise height, the accompanying stool, the tilt, and the illumination. It all had to exude an air of opulence that would deflect any second thoughts about its strategic placement.

He glanced at his watch; there were still twenty minutes before her arrival on her inaugural day, before she waltzed into the makeshift work area he had arranged in his office, a temporary fix until her permanent workspace was ready.

He had positioned the desk near the window. She had given off a vibe of endless summer, and he longed for the breeze to play with her locks, enhancing her allure in his eyes.

Another peek at his watch, then a quick adjustment to his three-piece suit. Perfection was the goal. A laptop awaited her, fresh flowers adorned one corner of the desk, and an elegant filing cabinet sat beneath. All within his line of sight. There, she would be visible in profile, while he, at forty-five, tried to tame the few resilient strands atop his glistening scalp.

This space was the antithesis of her essence. She had been a breath of fresh air during the interview, painting his imagination with her vivacious charm and sunny disposition. She was the beacon he craved after a drought of female presence.

Her profile stated she had just turned eighteen. Brown Rhonda—and the rest of her lengthy Brazilian name escaped him, tinged with an African lineage, something about adoption, he recalled vaguely. The interview details had blurred, overshadowed by her figure. Yet, since his brother-in-law bore the name Brown, a Frenchman he had little regard for, she would be Rhonda to him. A vibrant Latina he aspired to know intimately, to infuse this sterile place with a feminine essence. Yet, there was one vital role still vacant in the office, a role tailored just for him, and he believed she was the ideal fit.

A rap at the door.

Jeff straightened, adjusting his tie yet again, settled his glasses, and inhaled deeply. Come in, he called, his breath held in anticipation.

The door swung open, and in glided Rhonda, her hips swaying enticingly.

Jeff's heart raced as he took in the sight of the uniform, he had chosen for her, delivered to her address, now hugging the contours she had provided. The heels added inches to her petite frame, highlighting her bare legs that he admired with an eager gaze.

Her calves sported a rich tan, muscular yet devoid of prominent veins, exuding strength. That strength carried through to her thighs, even more striking in appearance.

Dressed in the white mini-skirt he'd requested, she entered his office, her stocking tops barely peeking out. Her thighs, muscular and prominent, were mostly exposed, showcasing well-defined muscles he hadn't even known existed. As she walked, the substantial size of her thighs caused them to brush against each other.

The contours of her backside, the edges of its fullness, were just visible above her hips. Observing her was a fleeting experience, yet the impression of her physique lingered in his mind like the prolonged credits of a film.

Her toned midriff was on display, adorned with a belly ring, and the upper edge of her white lace garter belt peeked out from the skirt's waistband. She wore a white crop-top, sleeveless and ending just above her navel, with a plunging V-neck that revealed a glimpse of her white lace bra, enhancing her ample bust. A conspicuous necklace dangled into the valley of her cleavage, and her light blonde hair cascaded in waves down to her waist.

He was talking about the commute and the hazards of taking the tube in such attire, mentioning some unsavory encounters, but his focus was elsewhere. His gaze was fixed on her face, captivated by her bright blue eyes, high cheekbones, the small mole under her left eye, her delicate nose, and her full, glossy pink lips that revealed a perfect smile.

Her voice lifted at the end of her sentence, signaling a question, and Jeff scrambled for a response, finding himself at a loss for words.

Mr. Hurley? she inquired, leaning forward with a knowing smile, her arms behind her back, pushing her chest out.

He was visibly flustered, a warm flush spreading across his face. Yes? he managed to reply.

Is there anyone who drives to work who might be willing to give me a lift? she asked, shifting from side to side.

Uh, yes— he scratched his head —I can.

Thank you, Mr. Hurley.

Please, call me Jeff, he offered, wrapping an arm around her waist and pulling her into an embrace, careful to keep his hands away from the tempting curves of her backside.

She hugged him back, a bit apprehensively. We do hugs here, he reassured her, resisting the urge to explore further with his hands.

Every day? she asked, her chest pressing against him, her face nestled against his chest.

Of course, he replied, his fingers brushing through her hair.

That feels nice, she murmured.

You're my employee, but your well-being is my priority, he assured her, hands resting on her hips.

You're so sweet, she said, her hands on top of his, perhaps a tad wary of the proximity to her backside.

I don't think I've ever seen a more stunning woman, he confessed, hoping she wouldn't take offense.

Oh, gosh, she replied, moving in for another hug.

He took that as a positive sign and embraced her again, feeling the warmth of her body against his.

Thank you, Sir. That might not be strictly professional, but it's what I needed today after the commute, she said.

If you ever need a compliment, I'm here for you, he replied, ending the hug. Let me give you a tour, he suggested, placing an arm around her waist as they walked.

The office was dim and had a musty scent, but a candle at her desk gave it a cozy atmosphere.

What's this? she inquired, puzzled.

The new offices aren't ready yet, but I've set up this workstation for you in the meantime, he explained, drawing her closer.

The warmth from where her hip touched his side was palpable. This is quite convenient for your secretary, she said with a smile, appreciating his effort.

She approached the desk, bent to smell the roses, and he couldn't help but admire her figure.

I'm glad you like it, but wait until you see the best part, he said, moving behind her and wrapping his arm around her bare midriff, inadvertently pressing her against him as he guided her back.

Goodness, the sensation of her against him was so delightful that he inadvertently held her close for a moment longer than intended before gently guiding her along with him. We have something here that might be of use to you, he suggested, revealing a door behind his desk.

A hidden restroom?

Indeed, a remnant from the prior owners, but I saw no need to get rid of it, he explained as he ushered her in.

If that's the case, I believe my commute just got easier, she remarked, leaning over the bathroom counter to adjust her makeup.

Is that so?

Absolutely, I can jog here, and then, if it's alright with you, catch a ride home with you?

That seems like a sensible arrangement, he replied, trying to mask his eagerness at the thought of her showering right behind his office wall. We'll need a way to remember you're in there, though. The door doesn't lock.

I could sing, maybe?

That's a charming idea, but not practical during meetings.

Will the sound of the shower be an issue?

Not at all, I can handle that if it comes up, but singing is harder

to explain.

Perhaps I could place something on the doorknob?

Maybe your lingerie? It would be easy to hang there.

Why not just a towel?

We pride ourselves on our local lingerie and, besides, towel

cleaning costs add up.

And if it's just hanging there?

It could still end up on the floor and get soiled.

Ah, and cleanliness is a priority for you? she inquired, tactfully

addressing his personal hygiene without directly mentioning it,

and he was grateful for her delicacy.

In that particular case, yes, he said, eager for her to consent to

the idea of leaving her intimate apparel on the doorknob.

So, my thongs would be alright? she asked, catching on to his

line of thought.

He approached her from behind as she leaned over the counter, wrapping his arms around her midsection, pressing against her.

I may be your boss, but I want this to be a comfortable space for you. However, there are a few things I would insist on.

She turned and pressed back against him with a smile. My thongs, then, she said with a hint of seduction.

Shall we get you set up at your desk? he suggested, feeling her against the countertop, and it took all his self-control not to act on his impulses.

Sure, but I do enjoy your embraces, she replied, biting her lip.

You'll have no shortage of them, Rhonda.

He escorted her out of the bathroom, already plotting to interrupt her shower with the pretense of needing the restroom himself. He believed she was naive enough to fall for it.

Rhonda moved to her workstation and took a seat, her posture impeccable and her skirt tightly stretched over her form. Her silhouette was a sight to behold, every curve on display, and he didn't hesitate to approach and place his hands on her shoulders.

That feels nice, she murmured contentedly.

He enjoyed the massage just as much, admiring her figure and the proximity to her. The scent of her hair and perfume was intoxicating.

How was that? he inquired as he finished the shoulder rub.

I hope that's a regular thing while we work together. Your hands are so warm.

I'm happy to hear that, he said, assisting her up. Later, I'll walk you through our computer system. Ready to meet everyone else?

She nodded and matched his pace as he led her out, his hand resting on her hip. He noticed her careful steps, her unfamiliarity with the heels affecting her walk.

Apologies, she said, I'm not used to heels with all this..., gesturing to her curvaceous figure.

He smiled, understanding her predicament, as they made their way to meet the team.

Do you get pedicures? he inquired, unable to suppress the probing thoughts swirling in his mind.

How did you figure that out? she responded, her lips parting in surprise.

What if I told you I know everything about you? What if I said I had a detective look into you before I brought you on board? he teased.

Her complexion drained of color.

Jeff sensed the shift in her demeanor; she took his words to heart. Although his tone was clearly playful, she bought into it. I'm just kidding around.

Oh, that explains it, she replied, her cheeks warming with a blush.

Let's go introduce you to the team.

Truth be told, the team wasn't large. Just eight people. It was a modest enterprise by design. Aside from the young woman at his side, the next youngest was fifty. Rhonda was a much-needed addition, but it was he who would work most closely with her as he gestured for her to enter the office ahead of him. She embraced his description of the office as a welcoming place quite literally, hugging each new acquaintance, while the men seemed reluctant to release her as they pressed against her ample bosom.

When she hugged Rickson, the fifty-two-year-old IT specialist, his hands strayed to the smooth skin of her lower back, his fingertips grazing the upper curve of her stunning posterior.

Jeff couldn't help but notice her voluptuous backside. It was an impressive sight, round and full—a perfect blend of muscle and softness. He felt a surge of fortune at this sight.

He caught Rickson's gaze lingering there as well. It was clear they both appreciated her figure, especially how her skirt hugged her form.

It was great meeting you, Rickson. I'll be sure to come to you if I have any computer issues, okay?

Any excuse will do, Rickson replied, finally releasing her from the embrace.

I'll remember that, she said, taking Jeff's hand as he escorted her from Rickson's office, his arm naturally finding its way around her waist.

She moved with a captivating sway, her colleagues' gazes following the rhythmic motion of her backside and the gentle bounce of her cleavage as she navigated the office in her heels.

Jeff imagined their thoughts mirrored his own as the young woman pressed her body against his side.

Upon entering his office first, he couldn't help but lick his lips at the sight of her backside.

He forced his gaze upwards when she turned to face him, her smile spreading contagiously. What did you think of everyone? They're all single, aren't they? she asked directly.

Why do you say that? How could you tell?

They seemed a bit too eager around me, but it's fine. I tend to get that kind of attention.

You're quite an eye-catching young woman. They were probably just a bit overwhelmed.

And you weren't?

Uh—

I was surprised by the dress code, but I think it's pretty cute, she mentioned, slipping off her heels. Is it okay if I take these off?

Jeff glanced at her delicate feet, noting the pink nail polish and the ankle bracelet that added to their charm. If it makes you more comfortable, then sure. But let's keep everything else as per the contract, he replied.

Thank you, Sir, she said, allowing his arm to guide her to her workstation.

Oh, Rhonda, my dear Rhonda, the pleasure is all mine, he said, booting up her laptop as she settled in.

You're very kind to me, Sir.

For the moment, he thought as he ran his fingers through her soft blonde hair. Please, Rhonda. Call me Jeff.

Could you walk me through the software, Jeff? I'm not the best with computers.

That's alright. Your computer skills aren't why I hired you.

Then why did you hire me?

You really don't know? he probed, believing the reason to be self-evident.

I mean, I don't have much experience.

Maybe you have a different kind of experience, one that's more valuable to me than to others, he suggested, admiring her crossed legs, her thighs full and well-shaped. How could she be so curvaceously built?

What kind of experience?

He inquired if you had prior experience working alongside your father, correct? he asked, rowing rapidly to escape the predicament he found himself in.

Indeed, my father frequently took me to his workplace during my youth, where I assisted him with organizing his office, sorting files, and similar tasks.

Exactly, that's what I need. Someone who knows how to collaborate with me, not against me. And I'm in dire need of someone to put my life in order. Fortunately for me, I have you now.

Rhonda's smile shone so brightly he was nearly compelled to lean in and kiss her plump lips, but he quickly shook off the enchantment she cast over him.

Chapter 3

Jeff assisted her with logging into the necessary programs, casually brushing her skin with his fingertips. Everything was going smoothly until the continuous leaning over began to strain his back. Why don't you check your inbox? I've prepared some tasks for you.

Where are you headed?

Jeff settled into his chair, leaning back and observing her as she shifted in her seat. It's just my back. The angle earlier wasn't ideal for me.

And what angle suits you best? she asked teasingly, catching him by surprise.

That's not exactly professional, Rhonda.

Apologies, but I can offer a massage if it would help?

No need for a massage, he replied, raising his hand, yet appreciating her willingness to assist. But remember, you're more than just my secretary, you're my personal assistant.

Indeed, I am, she replied, her smile radiant.

Could you fetch me a coffee?

Certainly. Rhonda rose swiftly, impressing him with how quickly she slipped into her heels before departing the office.

Jeff reclined and waited, then waited some more, growing impatient as Rhonda did not return. He decided to investigate, aware that the coffee machine was quite a distance away and that she wasn't the most graceful in her heels, but the wait had extended beyond a reasonable amount of time.

And he found himself missing her presence already.

She was undeniably stunning.

Upon locating her by the coffee machine, engaging in light-hearted conversation with Dickson, the fifty-nine-year-old accountant who had his arm around her waist, Jeff felt a twinge of irritation. She laughed at his jokes, while nearby, Donald, the sales manager and now the second youngest in the office, couldn't take his eyes off the charming Rhonda.

Noticing Jeff's approach, Rhonda suddenly remembered her errand. Oh no, I completely forgot about your—

Don't worry about it, Jeff interrupted, preparing his own coffee while Dickson resumed his tale of a troublesome ex-wife and infidelity.

Really? Rhonda chimed in when needed, engrossed in Dickson's narrative yet seemingly unaware of his hand creeping up her backside.

Dickson was a sly, seasoned man, capitalizing on Rhonda's either tolerance or naivety to his touches, much like every other man in the office.

That's when I caught her, and the shameless woman blamed me, Dickson grumbled, visibly annoyed, drawing Rhonda in closer with a lustful gaze.

Rhonda, ready to get back to setting up your workspace? Jeff, clutching his coffee and her hand, whisked her away, his bold move earning envious stares as he confidently placed his arm around her waist, his hand resting on the curve of her backside.

Back in the office, Rhonda slipped off her heels, her figure a vision of grace. What did you think of Dickson and Donald?

Dickson peered into her eyes, almost begging, before attempting once more.

Dickson, please don't, she said, her breath becoming uneven. She knew she should be pushing him away, yet she found herself immobilized as his unwelcome fingers grazed her skin. He moved closer suddenly, his hand lifting to cradle her chin, his lips brushing against hers in a fleeting kiss.

Please, I don't want—

Dickson ignored her protests, planting a swift kiss on her lips before she could turn away.

Just one little kiss, and then you can return to your boss, he coaxed, dangling the coffee cup just out of reach. Damn, you're too gorgeous.

She tried to pull away. Dickson... stop... please, she pleaded, struggling against his advances.

Dickson drew her in and planted a fervent kiss on her lips. She found herself reciprocating, her lips joining his in a dance she wished to resist, especially with his foul breath mingling with her own. In spite of the inner voice that screamed it was wrong, her body betrayed her, igniting an unfamiliar desire for him.

She wriggled, attempting to escape his hold. Dickson, please, stop this, she gasped, momentarily freeing herself from the kiss.

But Dickson was insistent, seizing her face and merging their lips once again.
Her muffled protest vibrated against his mouth before she could pull away. Dickson—

Ignoring her plea, Dickson's passion escalated, pinning her against the coffee machine. His hand boldly claimed one of her ample curves.

In a state of panic, she fought to push him away, yet his strength was overwhelming. A conflicting part of her craved for his touch to encompass her completely. His hand momentarily left her, but the relief was short-lived as it found its way up her thigh, skimming the edge of her skirt.

Dickson's excitement was palpable as he indulged in a more intimate caress.

Desperately, she tried to fend him off, her body a chaotic mix of resistance and arousal under his invasive touch. His hands were relentless, alternating between her breasts and thighs, his fingers inching closer to her most private area.

You're quite the temptress, Rhonda. It won't be long before you're the talk of the office, especially looking like you do, he whispered between kisses.

This time, her body succumbed to the bizarre craving, and she managed to reach for the cup.

As she turned to pour the coffee, his proximity only heightened her vulnerability.

Your figure is incredible, Rhonda. So full, so perfect, he breathed out, his hands exploring her.

His tongue traced her neck, hands roaming from her chest to her posterior, until she finally overcame the overwhelming sensation and pushed his hand away while the coffee filled.

I said stop, she asserted, pushing back, seeking space.

But her attempt backfired. His hand slipped beneath her skirt, pushing her underwear aside, and his fingers invaded her. His touch was skilled, and despite her shame, she couldn't help but respond.

Was she really on the edge of climax because of him? She questioned her own reactions.

That's it, embrace it, he taunted, finding humor in her conflicted enjoyment.

She glanced around, thankful their secluded spot by the coffee machine hid them from coworkers. Please, no more, she pleaded with the man who continued to bring her to the brink of ecstasy.

The coffee's ready. I won't have the boss upset because of your distractions, he remarked, leaving her clinging to the counter, reeling from the climax he induced. We'll see if you give in tomorrow.

With a final, stinging spank, he departed, leaving her in a mix of humiliation and lingering arousal.

After composing herself for half an hour, she returned, her appearance slightly disheveled, her nipples evident beneath her top.

Why the delay? he inquired, accepting the coffee she handed him.

The guys, they're, well, very forward, she replied, her cheeks tinted with embarrassment.

What happened?

Chapter 4

Dickson... he said I could only have the coffee if I kissed him.

And did you?

It was the only way to get your coffee, she replied, settling back onto her stool.

But a simple peck doesn't take half an hour.

Okay, he may have outdone me with that machine, and while kissing, he might've inappropriately touched me, and...

And what else?

I'd rather keep that to myself.

Jeff offered a reassuring smile. He really shouldn't have behaved like that. I'll speak with him, he said, rising from his chair.

I think he's already gone.

Left so soon?

Um, isn't it overtime for us today? she inquired.

Glancing at his watch, Jeff was taken aback by how time had slipped away, and she was indeed correct. He then saw her fidgeting with her skirt and adjusting her top. An impish thought crossed his mind, perhaps inspired by the apparent advantage Dickson had gained with her. Rhonda, do you know the reason I asked for the lace items?

No, but I did wonder about the specificity, she replied, facing him.

It's because on days like today, when overtime has me worn out, I like to end the day by checking the quality of our merchandise. That's where you come in.

How so?

Strip down, let me see you only in the lingerie.

We didn't discuss this in the interview, did we?

However, it's mentioned in the contract you signed.

Is it?

Yes, it is. Didn't you read your contract?

Um... no, she confessed, her gaze dropping.

That wasn't very wise.

Just another blonde moment, she exhaled. Well, if that's the case, I suppose I have no choice, she sighed once more and stood up. She slid off her skirt and then removed her top.

Now, she was clad only in her lingerie and heels.

The lacy bra enclosed her large, firm double E-cup breasts. Their size made him briefly wonder if they were real, but they certainly were. Such perfection couldn't be man-made.

He was struck by the perfect figure before him, and as per her application, she had just recently come of age. Rhonda, growing up must have been tough, he said, empathizing with the burden and the unwanted attention she likely endured.

Growing up was hard, she acknowledged, and it doesn't seem like it'll get easier here after what Dickson did.

At least you look stunning.

I'm not sure. She fidgeted with her thong's lace. It feels a bit tight. Are you certain you ordered based on my measurements?

I might have opted for a smaller size, he admitted, as she looked annoyed. Jeff raised his hands in defense. Just to test the fabric's strength, and believe me, it suits you perfectly, he remarked, his eyes lingering on her figure.

That makes sense, she said, running her fingers through her hair, clearly uneasy.

Could you turn around? I'd like to see how the bra fits your back, he requested, gesturing with a circular motion.

Don't you test these products before finalizing them?

Typically, on mannequins. We're a modest local business. Our chance to test them affordably is on our female staff.

So, I play a significant role then, she said with a tentative smile, yet her inexperience was clear as she cautiously turned, pausing when her bare backside faced him.

Jeff had seen it before, even marked it, but now it appeared even more prominent, partly due to her posture. She seemed to be intentionally accentuating it for his gaze, and he took in the sight of her perfectly shaped form. The thong's straps were hidden between her cheeks, with only the top triangle and band visible.

Rhonda, sweetheart, come over here, he called out, gesturing for her to approach. With each step, her toned thighs hinted at her muscular strength, as she gracefully made her way to him and stood before his parted knees. You know, having you wear these gives us a unique benefit, he remarked, his hand tracing the curve of her athletic thigh.

In what way? she inquired.

It allows me to explore the practicality of these lingerie sets, he explained.

What do you mean by 'explore'?

Sit on my lap, he directed, and she hesitated, biting her lip.

This is quite an unconventional first day, she observed, yet complied, her curvaceous form settling onto him as he caressed her ample thighs and grasped her generous backside, which seemed both abundant and yet not nearly enough.

Working for me will always be out of the ordinary, but as long as we enjoy it, why should we care about the specifics? he mused.

That's a fair point, she replied, her smile masking any discomfort his forwardness might have caused. He admired her resilience and openness to his bold advances.

But his curiosity grew.

I'd like to feel the bra when it's fully occupied, he stated, leaning in closer. Looking up at her, he was almost in disbelief that he might have the chance to touch her so intimately.

Then go ahead, she encouraged him with a mischievous grin.

He couldn't resist any longer, and his hands found their way beneath her ample bust, pressing into the generous flesh. Oh, this is bliss, he murmured, his fingers sinking into her softness as he let out a satisfied groan.

With eager hands, he explored the expanse of her chest, his dark fingers traversing every inch of her smooth skin.

Rhonda was seething inside. Why hadn't she scrutinized the contract to avoid this humiliating situation? And how had he sensed her vulnerability? The result of her oversight: letting this man handle her so freely. She shuddered as his hands compressed her breasts, his grin widening, and yet part of her responded despite her indignation. She resolved to endure it and find some silver lining.

Jeff was insatiable, his grasp becoming firmer, his expression one of unadulterated desire.

As he persisted, she found herself responding with sighs and moans, pushing back against his hands. Despite her internal protests, she found a perverse pleasure in his rough touch.

How do they feel? she asked.

Amazing. So solid and full.

I was referring to the bra, she corrected him with a laugh.

Oh, of course, he replied, momentarily distracted. I'll need a more thorough examination to decide, he said, burying his face in her cleavage, which she willingly accentuated by holding his head.

Do they feel good? she probed.

Are we still discussing the bra? he joked, nibbling and savoring her.

My breasts, you jerk.

They're incredible. But I need to see how they look in the bra while being put to the test, he said, unbuckling his belt.

What do you mean?

You know what I mean. I have to ensure the product performs under every condition, and you're the ideal model for it.

But—

Down on your knees, he commanded, adjusting his chair for the right height.

Are you serious? You want me to—

It's outlined in your contract. You should've read it.

I can't believe I missed that, she said, her spirits deflating.

It'll be quick, and once a set is tested, you won't have to do it again, he reassured her, stroking her hair.

Fine, but let's make it quick.

\

Just a brief one, he agreed, dropping his trousers and boxers as she knelt before him.

Chapter 5

Oh that-Surprised? she asked, calming her reaction at the sight of his thick shaft pointing directly at her. I guess you can never judge a book by its cover, she said, lifting her huge breasts. Rhonda stepped forward and moved so that her upper half was hovering over his crotch, then she tilted so that his huge, tight, black cock parted in the abyss her large breasts had created. Then she stopped and met his gaze, letting her huge breasts slide down and surround his cock with as flawless softness as possible. OH! Jeff moaned and threw his head back as his cock throbbed with excitement. His cock twitched with excitement and he felt the fuel tanks in his balls begin to fill. I can't believe I'm doing this, Rhonda said, as if shocked by his decisions that brought her to her knees before him. If my friend finds out...What happens in this office stays in this office, he comforted her and she smiled. The massive cleavage suited this case perfectly and even though there were plenty of tits to fuck, his cock was ready to cum. Let your tits bounce up and down on my cock. Lift up the heavy doors, he ordered her, and she did. Her big tits bounced as she slid them up and down on his penis, pulling his foreskin up and down with her sensuality. Am I doing things the way you want? It was all her. She did it all and knew exactly how to handle a cock. Spit on the head, he ordered, and she grimaced and continued bouncing her tits until she finally gave in and literally spit a drop of sage on the head. Let her tits sprinkle her saliva on his cleavage and cock. I loved you until now, she said, glaring at him. I thought you might be nicer than you think, but you're just like Dickson, aren't you? Oh, I'm so much worse, he moaned, the endless sweetness driving him crazy, his cock twitching as she increased the speed.

This vision was somewhat addictive. Seeing the soft, smooth flesh of her firm breasts resist the penetration of his cock, her luscious breasts clenched around him as he increased his speed, leaning further and further forward until the tip of his cock touched his bottom lip. Oh my God-Jeff lifted his hips, surprising her as the head of his cock entered her mouth. Rhonda couldn't help but close her mouth around his head to satisfy her curiosity about how bad the smell was, and it was exactly as she expected. It smelled like bad cheese. Look at you, Jeff said, kissing her breasts and lips. Damn, you're made for dirt. Rhonda couldn't help herself and couldn't resist the smell of cheese as she sucked and swirled her tongue around the shaft. She lowered her head and examined his length more closely until her chin was tucked into her cleavage, pushed up by her bra. Jeff grabbed his head and ran his fingers through his hair, stroking it. Such a good girl, he said as she sucked his cock up and down. Look at me, darling. Looking into his eyes for the first time in several minutes, he brushed her hair out of her eyes so he could, she released his cock from her mouth and ropes of sticky saliva connected them both. It was fun, but don't you think it's a little late? she asked, looking a little nervous as she stood up on shaking legs. Of course, you're right, I just got carried away. It's okay, I'm used to it, she said and he surprised her by grabbing her shapely thighs and lifting her up until he was pushing her against the desk. Jeff, what are you doing? I need to see how they affect performance, he said, putting his hand on her thong. Her big blue eyes widened and she sat up on her elbows. Do you mean that seriously? She asked as he pushed her thong aside. I'm not sure I want this, Jeff. He's already gone, I think he's gone too far. There is no going back now, my love. She tried to take a step back and out of his reach, but he grabbed her by his incredible thighs and pulled her back. By quickly adjusting the standing desk, it was in the perfect position.

Please, I'm not comfortable with this. I had a boy...It doesn't matter, he said, lifting his head from the mushroom. Can't we talk about the contract again? So damn sexy, he said as he pressed the mushroom head against her shaved pussy lips. Please, I don't want to-Jeff pushed his black cock inside her. This can't be happening, she said as his thick rod stretched her tight pussy. I think the same thing, he said, struck by her beauty as she lay on her back, her blonde hair framing her pretty face. Her eyes were closed and her thick pink lips were parted and moving slightly as she grimaced, panted and grunted in time with his first thrusts. God, she was so beautiful, perfect in every way, and she let her new boss, an old pig, fuck her teen pussy on her first day while wearing the company's sexy lace lingerie. It was an absolute coup de grace for the former office whores who benefited from them in the workplace. Rhonda was simply made for sex, as her tight, wet pussy said, clasping his body, massaging his girth, making each inch go further than the last. You're wearing a condom, aren't you? I didn't even think about it, he said as he thrust deep into her pussy. Fuck, you can't cum in me, he moaned. Why not?I don't take the pill and my boyfriend and I…It's okay, he said, not wanting to do anything that could ruin this incredible luck he had. Instead, I will use this opportunity to test the underwear further. What do you mean? I'll get out just in time and cover your panties in cum. Look how beautiful it is. Okay, that sounds better, she agreed, hell, she accepted him covering her in cum. Oh, that's so...ugh.... great, Rhonda murmured. Jeff usually didn't like office sluts when he fucked them for the first time, but with such a beauty moaning in pain as he thrust and penetrated her tight pussy, his motivation was destruction. I low it is?

So big, she moaned, covering her cum-filled face with her hands, panting and crying. I have a boyfriend, she said crying as he straightened up and pushed in, shaping her pussy to fit him and not the pathetic loser waiting for her at home. And you betray him, he described the reality. I never wanted that, she said, wiping away her tears. Then why don't you use it, he said, running his hands over his broad thighs, the muscles of which felt wonderful, and stopped. Rhonda removed her hands, her eyes were no longer covered in cum and she looked really pissed. You know why, great man! Since you're a blonde sissy, sign up to be my personal sex toy, he said with a big smile. I'm not going to be your damn toy! Rhonda moaned and slammed her head against the cum covered desk as he built up a pleasant rhythm. He thrust into her relentlessly, increasing power and speed with each re-entry into her deepest regions. Jeff soon began fucking her brutally. He shuddered at the sight of her cum-covered breasts, shaking as he penetrated her, feeling the spasm of her pussy and milking his cock for maximum pleasure. Jeff moaned, the disgusting feeling of this beauty's pussy squeezing his thick, throbbing cock was what he lived for. God, he loved watching his white cock pound into the delicious little Latina. Oh... Rhonda sighed. I can feel it... so fucking deep, she groaned, her face contorted in pleasure and pain. Deep enough? he asked, his hips a blur as he ploughed her pussy. Please, I don't think I can take any more... You will, he said and continued thrusting, feeling her pussy resisting his passage, as muscular as it was, it had never been there before. Oh my God! Rhonda sighed and wrapped her legs around him as he pressed his hips against her thighs. Jeff wrapped one around his legs, enjoying the unusual shape before continuing his walk. She was beautiful. Her curvy body moved under his thrusts, and those massive, jiggly double E cups tantalized him as he pounded her youthful pussy hard.

HIT!

He patted her tits and dug his fingers into her hard, round breasts, squeezing them just as hard as he fucked her.

SPANK!

It hurts...Rhonda moaned and raised her head to watch the action as he slapped her bra covered breasts left and right.

SLAP!

I said-

SPANK!

Oh, please-

SPANK!

It's not a C...

SLAP!

It's-

SPANK!

I'm the one trying this, he reminded her, squeezing her big tits, and I need to see how they hold up.

SLAP!

Jeff grabbed the lace bra by the ties that connected the cups and ripped it off.

Oh, you're crazy!

SPANK!

Her large naked breasts swayed freely on his chest as he discarded her bra.

SPANK!

Oof! Female dog! Big pig! She moaned and her body almost shook as his cock stroked her nicely.

You like rough sex, don't you? Jeff asked with a knowing smile as he squeezed her big tits and fucked her like crazy.

Why do you ask? He groaned and didn't meet his gaze.

Come on, admit you want it.

I want to finish this!

I can't let that happen, at least not yet. Jeff acted quickly, lowering the desk to the optimal height for her to climb, lifting her heavy legs until her little feet dangled over his shoulders, and pushed himself forward in front.

Easy! She screamed as he folded her in half and leaned over her, looking him straight in the eyes while his beer belly rested against her toned stomach, holding her in place.

Now let's try out this Latina pussy, he said as he pushed down, pulling it out and pushing it in. He fucked her with slow, deep, hard strokes that made her jaw drop and her eyes roll deeper into the back of her head. Jeff saw it in her, the advantage of the angle, the extra length that had entered her. You like it, don't you? A guy has never made you so angry, has he?– he asked again, his body working smoothly, pushing his entire length into her again and again.

Ahhhh! - he shouted, tensing his body and shaking his head. Her massive breasts swayed lewdly as he pushed his hips against her, her large breasts slapping against his chin.

My God, they were so big that he had to feel them again. He pushed his legs forward until his ankles were near his ears. Hold her, he ordered, grabbing both of her bare breasts and the naughty little girl grabbed her legs to maintain the angle that was best for him. Rhonda's body shook against him, her moans sounding like a broken record player and frequent as he pushed his cock into her, his scrotum slapping loudly against the back of her thighs. Oh no... It cannot be...I'm coming! She cried out as the climax rocked her and her eyes lit up. Ahhhh! You're fucking me too hard! It's too deep! AHAHAHH!! This is just foreplay, Rhonda, he groaned as he smiled at her and squeezed her jiggling breasts to his liking.

Oh man! She moaned and closed her eyes as her whole-body shook, vibrations and pleasure exploding through her and he could see the pleasure on her face. She loosened her ankles and dug her long nails into his shirt, tearing it apart as she squirmed and lost control of herself.

Just keep fucking me! She screamed, her body exploding with pleasure, and he felt his heart beneath his hands, beating rapidly as his system seemed to shut down.

I'll make you something better, he said, releasing her breasts to find her clitoris. He wanted her to completely give up trying to control her wildness.

AAAAAAAAAAAAAAAAAAAAAAAAAAAAAAAAAAAAAAAAAAAAAAAAAAAAAAAAAAAAAAAAAAAAAAAAAAAAAAAAAA! He screamed at the top of his lungs, his body trying to shake him violently and his legs flying away in an attempt to escape his control. TO STOP! AHAHAHA!!! HEY AB!!! OH MY FUCKING GOD!!! AHAHAHA!!!

Jeff loved it, she was so wild and at the same time he was afraid to penetrate her dirty side even more and he wouldn't let her escape. He left her lying there, playing with her clit and continuing to drill her pussy.

AAAAAAHHHHH! She continued to scream, her pussy convulsing around his cock, squeezing it and drenching it with her juices as he pulled it out of her pussy.

Shit. Jeff had never seen a woman come on his cock like that and he couldn't remember anyone having as much fun as this little slut.

Fuck you! Fuck you! Fuck you! She demanded more and screamed wildly, and he was glad his office was soundproof. None of the other firms, below and above their floor would know what he was doing. Only he got to listen to her singing.

Sing for me, Rhonda. He reached up and placed his hand atop her cheekbone.

SLAP!

OOOOOHHHHH SSSSHHHHHIIIITTTTT!! She moaned loudly as she squirted her juices, soaking his pants and creating a waterfall on his desk.

CLICKS!

SING!

AAAAHHHHHH!!! MMMmmmmmhhhhhppffff! Jeff had to kiss him, harnessing his passion and pleasure and letting her tongue and lips go wild on him with the hottest, most fiery kisses he had ever received. She was wild, her hands grabbing a few strands of his almost bald head and almost tearing them away as she kissed back forcefully.

Mmmmmmhpppppppfffff! She moaned into his mouth as her body continued to convulse and juices flowed from her trembling body.

When she stopped moving and shaking, he broke their kiss and moved away from her so she could move her legs. Rhonda's big ass slammed against the desk, the last of her juices squirting out of her as she lay beneath him, panting and glistening with sweat, her lips swollen from the force of their desperate kisses.

That was... I need.... Please...let me breathe, she pleaded for a chance to regain her strength, but Jeff wouldn't stop.

Take it! He resumed the action, fucking her hard and fast. As Jeff began drilling her again, his eyes immediately went to her huge breasts, which were shaking under his powerful thrusts. Fuck, I love your big tits, he said, diving in to capture the nipple in his mouth.

Really? Damn, I didn't notice. Rhonda grabbed his head and wrapped her legs around his back. Jeff alternately fingered her nipples as she pressed him against her perky breasts, his sage covering her tanned, sweaty skin as his hands squeezed and caressed her perfection. You have great tits, he moaned and continued sucking them.

You old bastards still like my tits, she sighed and moaned as he bit one nipple and twisted the other. – Why are you so good at it? she asked, moaning as he licked her out and continually pushed into her wet pussy.

I already had big breasts, but they were old and saggy. I've never had young breasts as big and firm as these, he said, biting her nipple.

And you'll have her every day, she said, pulling his head so their eyes met, all because of this stupid contract.

You reap what you sow, he smiled at her and raised himself up on his elbows, looked at her, grabbed her head and slapped him in the face.

And when will you receive your reward?

Why?

Because he forced me to cheat on my boyfriend.

Did Dickson force you to cheat too?

He didn't fuck me-

He did it with his fingers.

It was different.

How? Didn't he let you come?

Shut up and fuck me harder, she ordered him and he happily

obliged.

Ah, I don't think I need this contract, he boasted.

Fuck me and shut up! She moaned and panted, visibly

preparing for another orgasm.

I think I'll let you come back, Rhonda. Sensing this, she quickly

moved her legs back and put her hands behind her knees to

restore the position, and he was happy to help her. He's just...

so affected...ok, she moaned as he set her down so her big ass

was in the air, her big tits were resting on his chin and his cock

was pressed against her sweet spot.

Chapter 6

You're learning now, Rhonda, he said, smiling at the damn toy he was making for the office. Imagine those years. If you leave, you'll become a sex addict...when you leave our office.

Oh man! She cried out loudly, the thrusts and his words brought her significantly closer to the edge. She went crazy again.

Do you like the idea of being my fuck toy, Rhonda? – he asked her, tensing up more and more and concentrating all his efforts on eliciting a bold scream from the Latina.

Rhonda's beautiful eyes closed as waves of pleasure washed over her face and her body soon began to tremble.

Jeff gave it to her again and again and her juices flowed out and coated the shaft. He kept going, pounding the pussy again and again at the same perfect angle.

Oh my God! I can feel it! Rhonda groaned, still closing her eyes and shaking her head.

Take my big fat cock, my slut, and cum!

OH GOD! Rhonda moaned, her body dripping with sweat. Jeff pounded her hard, sinking her deeper into prostitution with each thrust. Scream at me, my bitch!

OHHHHH EEEEEESSSS! - She screamed. You're going CUUUUUMMM!!! AHHHHH!!!

Do it! Do it! Do it! Jeff growled and drove into her again angrily. Ah! Uh! Ah! Rhonda screamed, her ears hurting from the volume and her body exploded as she sprayed her juices again. Cum for me, slut, he urged, as this orgasm seemed weaker than the others and her body was tired from the constant destruction, he was subjecting her pussy to. Don't stop… she sighed, falling back onto the desk. Her big ass made a loud noise as her heavy, round cheeks pressed together and her juices formed another waterfall that enlarged the pool under the desk. She looked exhausted, excited and in desperate need of rest.

But Jeff showed her no mercy and started fucking her hard again.

No... no... NOT...I need to rest... you can't...

CLICKS!

What can't I do? He asked as she grabbed his cheekbone, which had turned red from the impact.

How are you going to get over me? Should I be the youngest? – she asked shocked that he hadn't come yet and was still fucking her.

If you're going through the same thing as me, darling, he began, eliciting a moan from her, age is just a number.

Jerzy. She sighed and then remained silent as he brutally fucked her.

That big ass kept pounding the desk as her pussy adjusted and warmed up to his cock and her walls seemed ready for more. She had so much potential and he wanted to make her the perfect sex toy. – she begged with fear in her eyes because she probably felt the same way as he did. She was close to orgasming again, her body now in control and her mind ephemeral as it worked on her pussy like a wonderful tool.

Milked her orgasm like he was squeezing her breasts.

Then it exploded again.

Oh my God, oh my God, oh my God! Her eyes rolled back in her head, her head fell back onto the desk and she panted rapidly as he fucked her faster and harder. He drills it into his little slut. AAAAHHHH!!!ICH BIN CUUUUMMMMMIINNNGG!! AHAHAHA!!

«Hey! He liked it, he felt the rhythm of life inside her and tried to follow the beat of her heart and let her reaction to this obscene fuck set the pace.

Your cock feels great! My boyfriend would never do that! She moans and feeds her ego as she looks at him with teary eyes. And then...

She stood up and tried to kiss him, but couldn't reach his lips... So, he jumped in and met her halfway. Her kisses were wild and he liked to think that was her way of thanking him. That she was a slut who took control and let him know that she was impressed and that she liked what he was doing to her.

Finally, her lips parted in a passionate sigh and strands of sage connected her parted lips.

Then he surrounded him with his limbs and pressed their breasts together. Thank you, she moaned in his ear as he rammed his balls deep and hard against her ass. Don't you dare stop fucking. I need more! Oh my God, Rhonda, he began, biting her earlobe as he pressed her large breasts under his chest. What a whore you are.

Don't tell anyone, she moaned, giggling in his ear. Just let me come back.

Oh, I feel like you're getting closer! Jeff groaned, the slut's pussy gripping him so tightly that a shiver of desire ran through him. At this point he sped up and rubbed harder against her hot Latina.

Are you coming closer?

Oh, I'm fighting now, he admitted, wishing it would never end, but she held him too tightly. Her body was too beautiful not to cum in, but he had to respect her wishes. He couldn't ruin everything... Not yet.

As long as you put me first. I need to feel that feeling again. Please help me...please help me, he begged.

Rhonda collapsed onto the desk, pulling him close and pressing their lips together as he fucked her to another orgasm. His moans reached her mouth as she held him there, dancing with her tongue.

Jeff returned the kiss and slammed her against the desk. He heard the desk making strange noises. He had never broken a desk before, but the noise probably suggested that.

Damn, what a whore, and he hadn't even come yet despite fucking her so hard.

Their naked, sweaty bodies stuck together with sweat and limbs as they fucked and kissed like crazy. That's exactly what happened, they had climaxed together. He had to warn her, he wasn't taking pills, and at his young age, having just turned eighteen, there was a good chance that his thick, strong thighs could hold him inside her.

He knew, he felt it, that if he didn't find a way to free himself from her endless kisses and powerful thighs, he would be finished. It would be a one-time thing and he would never fuck her in the ass.

He was a moment away but couldn't move. She had incredible stamina, but her body held the strength and she was lost, lost in filth and pleasure. Her juices

He spurted against his cock as he became a piston machine, fucking her to the edge. And his whole body was shaking.

She had an orgasm and he was right behind her.

Jeff moaned and couldn't stop himself from fucking her harder and harder. She was just amazing, he had to keep fucking her, then he found a solution to free himself from her grip when the cum was about to leak out. He grabbed her throat and squeezed the tube, choking her, biting her tongue lightly and pressing his elbow into her chest.

Rhonda screamed into his mouth but recovered from the shock and he let go and pulled out, slamming into her orgasmic body.

Shit! Crap! Crap! Jeff moaned and squirted inside her, splattering her body with cum as her juices flowed out.

cum landed directly on his face, ropes of cum turning his tanned skin white and covering his nose, cheekbones and forehead as he tripped over the office scales. As a result, his cum flowed over the rest of her body, ropes of cum connecting her chin to her big tits as he covered her and her toned stomach in hot, sticky white cum.

And when he had not finished, he arose and knelt before his face.

Oh! – he groaned as he tensed his balls, this ball landed directly on his eyelid and collected a large amount there, part of which connected to his smooth, parted lips and the rest landed on his neck.

Rhonda then surprised him and grabbed his cock with both hands, opening her mouth and sticking out her tongue as she jerked him off and shot a shower of cum into his mouth like a real dirty slut.

His tongue stuck out, full of cum, and a puddle gathered in his mouth, overflowing with cum until it gurgled and he had to swallow.

Jeff fell and sat on her breasts, supporting them with his hands on his massive thighs so as not to crush them. But his cock wouldn't stop pulling, and she grabbed it with her tongue and swallowed it while he mustered the strength to get up and leave the office.

Jeff grabbed the desk and leaned over her as she stood, panting from her powerful climax, his eyes enjoying her work. Rhonda lay on her back covered in cum, her body glistening with sweat and her tongue hanging out as she panted and fed on the excess cum that covered her front and face.

Shit, I can't see, he said, his eyes closed in the sticky cum.

Chapter 7

Jeff had never seen a hotter sight and his cock hardened at the sight. He took off his tie and shirt and quickly undressed until he was back to his full height.

You don't have to see it, he said, walking around the desk, grabbing her ankles and pulling her down until she could stand.

How? he asked, narrowing his eyes as he saw the massive cock twitching at his mere presence. – How hard are you still?

Thank you, he said, turning her heavy body, the thickness of her ass visible to his eyes as he held her exactly where he wanted her. She bent over the desk at waist level, showing off her thong-clad cheeks. to him.

RUN!

It's time for the big moment, he said, thrusting into her, her vaginal muscles clamping down on his shaft and doing the impossible, holding him in place and even increasing his hardness as he moved fully back into her tight embrace.

RUN!

Oh, at least let me rest! She screamed as he grabbed her hair and lifted her upper body.

RUN!

Under her chin he could see her large breasts jiggling with each thrust into her huge ass, and her blue eyes looked up at him dreamily beneath all the cum filling her. – Isn't it a little too late? – he asked with a groan.

I think I've been fucking you for a long time, but I don't plan on stopping.

But I think it might be a boy-

RUN!

Maybe-

RUN!

I'm starting to suspect-

RUN!

That's what I do-

RUN!

Something like…

RUN!

I like…

RUN!

That! he groaned, and they both managed to get the phone on his workstation to vibrate. But she still remained bent over the desk, her back arched and her eyes on him as he pounded her ass. Eager for more and to experience more of its intoxicating beauty.

Maybe you should think about your boyfriend before you sign the contract?

RUN!

Oh, so deep, she moaned as he plowed her.

RUN!

Instead, you have to cheat on him every day after work, in the sexy lingerie we have, and soon...Maybe you even want my sperm inside you.

RUN!

Oh, you're such a bastard, Jeff.

RUN!

An evil, fat, dirty bastard who makes stupid girls ..

RUN!

Your-

RUN!

Shit!

RUN!

Jeff threw her onto the desk and slammed her ass while cum

dripped from her face and forehead onto her desk. Are you the

one behind this beauty? A whore?

RUN!

I'm not-

RUN!

Your whore-

RUN!

Such a whore, but not mine.... again, he teased.

KILLING!

Oh, shut up!

RUN!

You'll be my whore too, he said, fucking her so hard that she

gasped and moaned in pain.

RUN!

I'm only doing this because you cheated on me-

RUN!

That doesn't define me-

RUN!

He will do it.

RUN!

Oh, you-

RUN!

Damn big bite…

RUN!

I hate it!

RUN!

Why is your body getting it? Why are you allowing it?

RUN!

Shut up!

RUN!

That dirty mouth makes me want you even more.

RUN!

Will you stop hitting me?

RUN!

Ass!

RUN!

Jeff…

RUN!

It fucking hurts!

RUN!

And you love him, don't you?

RUN! KILLING!

Oh man…

RUN!

Yes!

RUN!

That's what this ass was made for!

RUN!

Built for abuse!

RUN!

My aggression!

RUN!

Only when I wear your underwear, she corrected him.

RUN!For now, she said, pushing her hair back so she could look

at the cum stuck to her face.

RUN!

You're fucking disgusting, she growled at him.

RUN!

What the hell, kitten, he said, laughing at her attitude.

RUN! As she recovered from her orgasm, she rolled her eyes and the more he slapped her chubby cheeks, the louder she moaned.

RUN!

Oh, please-

RUN!

I can't breathe... she gasped as he fucked her silly.

RUN!

I can't-

RUN!

Br-

RUN!

Then let me help you, he said as he grabbed her mouth, his fingers slipped into her mouth and spread them wide apart, using them as handles so he could pound her harder and faster, and she transformed into a scream and a sketch. Disturbance.

Arghhhh! Arghhhh! Arghhhh!She screamed, tears streaming down her fingers as he drilled into her hot flesh.

Fuck, take it, Rhonda. Get all the customs!

Argghhh! Arghhh! Rhonda's body went limp, her strong legs giving out and her arms dangling at her sides as she moaned and groaned in his embrace.

Jeff released her mouth and helped her fall onto the desk, forcing her head down. She leaned back and moaned on the desk, her large breasts pressed together and overflowing on either side as he neared orgasm.

RUN!

Argggh!

RUN!

I'm going to cover this ass in cum!

RUN!

Arrghhhh!

RUN!

Damn, what a damn body!

DASH!

Arggghhhh!

RUN!

There it is, bitch. It's fucking happening!he roared, pressing his thighs onto the desk, pulling out and letting his cum run down her back. It moved up her back, clung to her hair, touched the side of her face that faced the blanket, ran into her blue eyes, and some even touched the flesh of her breasts that were overflowing beneath her, but most landed on his Butt.

Jeff fell backwards, his poor balance causing him to quickly fall into the chair he was sitting in and watch as his juices flowed out.

Rhonda lay on the desk, her bruised ass full of cum and her chest gasping for air. Arghh, she moaned in pain, and between the expressions of pain came a soft moan that he didn't want to hear, he just wanted to hear it. Everything was important. She stayed bent over the desk for a good twenty minutes until a muscle twitched.

I don't think you can walk into your boyfriend's house looking like that, Jeff said, squeezing his trembling thighs.

I have to take a shower, he whispered, his voice barely audible.

Shit, you've never been fucked so well, have you? Jeff regained hope. He looked completely destroyed. Never, he admitted with a groan, but he was too weak to hide it now. He hated to admit that it was written all over his twisted face. He loved every moment and hated himself for it.

RUN!

Ah, she screamed as the cum flowed into her ass.

RUN! KILLING!KILLING!

cum leaked out of her ass as she shook and fell onto the desk as her juices flowed out of her.

RUN!

Come here, Rhonda. He grabbed her hair and lifted her up.Let me clean up the mess I made. Water splashed on her skin, her shapely curves rippled and her feet slipped and spread as she arched her back and looked into his eyes as he fucked her huge ass from behind.

DASH!

Oh damn, he groaned, wondering what it looked like from his perspective. He could see her large breasts pushed under her chin, or his gaze was focused solely on her large buttocks moving under his powerful thrusts.

RUN!

A stream of water hit her face and she held her mouth open as he turned the shower head and washed the dirt from her battered body.

RUN!

Why are you…

RUN!

Shit…

RUN!

Me?

RUN!

Oh my God!

RUN! Because it is a sufficient opportunity to test the water resistance of the underwear, he said, continuing to abuse the technical details of his contract to the limit.

RUN!

I'm going to have an orgasm, she finally admitted openly, so he knew she wanted more.

RUN!

You big, dirty pig...

RUN!

I'm going to cum on your ugly, disgusting mushroom cock!

RUN!

Cum for me, Rhonda.

RUN!

I'm so close.

RUN!

Come on me.

RUN!

That's me...aaahhhh! »

RUN! KILLING!

Cum for me, darling.

RUN!

Please stop fucking me, he begged

RUN!

No chance! I'm still testing your underwear.

RUN! Rhonda's incredible thighs shook and trembled and rippled as he slammed hard into her. She tried to speak, the stream of water washing the cum from her face and her moans silencing her every time she opened her mouth.

RUN!

What is this…

RUN!

Oh, stop it!

RUN!

AHHH! She moaned in shock as he slapped her ass.

RUN! KILLING!

Oh! he groaned again.

RUN!

Jeff took great pleasure in spanking his big ass. It was a perfect work of art, an ass designed to be spanked, punished and destroyed by hardcore fucking. It was just incredibly thick and strong.

RUN! KILLING! KILLING!

Mmm! She moaned, trying her best to suppress a loud moan because her boyfriend had never done anything like that to her before and the pleasure coursing through her was insane. He's never felt anything like this before. Everything he did to her drove her crazy, and it all depended on how terrible it was. It should have been.

DASH!

Jeff pulled back her beautiful blonde hair and pushed his big cock further into her tight teen pussy. His eyes were forced to look straight ahead as he knocked her unconscious.

AAAHHHHHHHHHHHH!

FFFFFFFFUUUUUUUUUUCCCCCCCKKKKKK

RRREEEEEEESSSSSSSSSSSSS! – she cried as a shiver of desire ran through her.

RUN!

OH! Fuck me, you big slut! Fuck me hard! OH YEAH! OHHH!Wow! » She moaned loudly again as the water splashed on her body. Oh yeah! You're so damn good, you disgusting piece of trash! So great!Damn, damn! OH!

RUN!

AHHH! Yes!– he screamed with joy and penetrated him harder. RUN! KILLING!

UGHHH! Shit, shit, shit!– she moaned as he repeated the action.

RUN! KILLING!

As she explored her surroundings, the tanned blonde slut was bent over at the waist, impaled on his thick eight inches, screaming for his cock as her big ass cheeks heaved under his powerful thrusts.. Jeff has never felt more like a man. Making this beauty scream on his cock was an incredible feeling that he couldn't get enough of.

RUN! KILLING!

AHHHH! Haha! YES! YES! – she screamed in pleasure, her pussy pulsating around his swollen cock.His cock slowly slid into her, covered in her pussy juices, his balls slapping against her. Once inside, he ran his hand over her red bottom, teasing her with his hand as he filled her luscious ass. Finally, after moments of teasing...

RUN! KILLING!

UGGGHHHH! I love it! I fucking love it! she moaned, her body burning with wicked pleasure. Then he grabbed her hips again, fucking her even harder, making her curse with pleasure. Ahhh!

UGHHH! GOD! Pooh! Pooh! I UNDERSTAND! Seeing how much she enjoyed this harsher treatment, he slid a hand down her back, reached up to tuck it into her blonde hair, balled it into his fist, and pulled her back.

AHHHHH! YES! YES! JUST DO IT! Treat me like a fucking whore! YES! She cried out loudly, covering her eyes with her hand as her head bent into his kisses, nose pointed toward the ceiling as he pounded her mindlessly.

GOD! YES! DAMNED! Do whatever you want with me! Yes! he groaned.

Shit! Female dog! Damn good! » he moaned and spit into her open mouth, then he bent down and kissed her, savoring her plump, pink lips.

MMMMMHHPPPFFFF! She moaned into his mouth and arched her entire body against him as they attacked her like animals.

Jeff fucked the blonde from behind as their tongues danced and their bodies collided in rough sex.

Shit! Cholera! He groaned and pushed himself even harder into her tight kiss, his cock blurring as she pounded his ass. Jeff continued kissing him, loving the taste of her lips.

AHHHH! YES! Oh my God! YES! That's right! YES! YES! Uh!AHHHH! She moaned and her pussy quivered on his shaft.

UGGHHH! GOD! YES! YES! he shouted.

Jeff pushed her forward, grabbed her hair with both hands and dragged her to the base. He leaned back and thrust into her as she screamed in pain and pleasure. A concert of kindness that was echoed by the applause of her perky breasts and massive buttocks. He couldn't believe he was about to orgasm again, but he was quickly getting closer. She was too perfect.

I'm close, Rhonda.

Can you please not penetrate me? he begged for mercy.

There are only two places I can place inside you.

Not in my ass! You are too tall. You're going to tear me apart.

But here I want to fulfill you, he said, taking his hand out of her hair.

RUN!

Don't you fucking dare say that...

RUN!

Jeff pulled the mushroom head out as she strolled and pressed it against her sphincter, which wasn't as tight as it should have been. Apparently, it had been repaired today, probably by her boyfriend, but now she was going to make this hole her own.

RUN!

Oh man, you're huge!

RUN!

Taller than your boyfriend, I take it?

KILLING!

Shut up!

RUN!

You have to stop hitting me…

RUN!

This might take some abuse, he said, pushing against the initial resistance of her ass.

RUN!

Oh my God! Whore… moaned the blonde, feeling the thick pillar pressing against her tightest hole. And he didn't give up without a fight, resisting her relentless weapon. Finally, her tight asshole gave in to the intense pressure he was applying to his huge fuck hole. , spreading himself apart wide and swallowed the entire head of his big cock. Ohhh! Whore! FUCK! she screamed in pleasure as her anus stretched around his shaft.

RUN!

Jeff moaned, his cock experiencing a whole new tension.

Shit! SHIT! She screamed as he pushed his cock deeper into her, his girth covered in her juices and water so he could slide in easily.

RUN!

OH FUCK! FUCK!» – the blonde screamed in pleasure, her asshole twitching in pleasure as she welcomed the next few inches of his throbbing cock. Damn, you're so fat! And you're going to do this to me every day?

RUN!

Every day, he said, placing his hand on his favorite thing in the world.

RUN!

Shit!

RUN!

Jeff smiled widely as he pushed his cock further into Rhonda's ass.

RUN!

Oh my God! Female dog! Female dog! Cholera! gasped the sexy Latina as her asshole pulled out his swollen cock.DAMN IT! he groaned. Keep it up! I can handle anything! YES!She moaned, but he continued, not stopping until he bottomed out inside her, her anus now wrapped tightly around the base of his shaft.

RUN!

UGGGGHHHH! GGGGDOBRADDDDDDDDD! FUCK!– she moaned, the pleasure making her moan as she held her legs open. Her toes were the only contact she had with the floor as her legs bent and shook to keep her ass at the perfect angle for fucking.

RUN! Jeff moaned loudly and pushed his hand into her perfect ass, and as she held that position her ass and legs tensed and stuck out and he almost saw it. She was incredibly fit and well built.

RUN!

Oh fuck! She moaned as he spanked her and grabbed her hips, fucking her faster and holding her still as he slammed her in pain and pleasure.

RUN!

OH FUCK YOU! She screamed, her head bowing in shame, but with each thrust into her ass he saw her smile overcome the shock and fill her shame with pleasure.

RUN! This ass is mine now, Jeff said, grabbing her by the hair that reached her hips. It was so sweet and juicy, just like her, and it was beyond adorable. It was instinctive. A purge to multiply it and ensure no one else has access to it.KILLING!

Say it!

RUN! KILLING!

Say you're mine!

RUN! KILLING! KILLING!

Forget your friend! He's not the one driving you crazy!

RUN! KILLING! KILLING!

I can't take it anymore! Please--

RUN!KILLING! KILLING!

Tell me you would rather be here with me than with him!

RUN! KILLING!

FUCK YOU! she screamed as he fucked her rougher, harder

and faster.

SPANK!

Say I'm better!

SPANK!

I can't-

RUN!

Tell me I'm better than him!

RUN!

Here you go!

RUN!

Good dog! Jeff smiled as she looked up at him, her eyes shining

with lust and lust, her tongue sticking out, sage dripping from it

as she fucked his eyes.

RUN!

Tell me you'd rather me fuck you than him!

RUN!

You're fucking crazy! She screamed and gargled with her own saliva, enduring the pain his asshole was inflicting on her.

RUN!

Tell me you'd rather be with me!

RUN!

Admit it!

RUN!

And damn it say it!

RUN!

YES!!!! She screamed, her big legs shaking, her butt lifting from his thrusts, her back arched and he could see her big breasts bouncing under her chin. But her eyes stared at him before rolling to the back of her head as he kissed her silently, his tongue sticking out of her mouth as he grabbed her by the throat, choking her as hard as he pushed her back. HairMy boyfriend would never do that!

Hearing that, he filled her asshole to the brim and sent his cum deep into her tightest hole while spitting into her mouth just for pleasure. Feeling like a king who did whatever he wanted with her. The only respect he showed her was not to dump her, even though he could have easily done that. Thank you, he whispered in her ear, overcome with emotion as he realized how much she had allowed him to make love, for better or worse.Filling her ass with cum sent him over the edge and he pulled back, leaning against the shower stall while she leaned against the other with her arms outstretched for support.

KILLING!

Oh, stop it!

RUN!

It's so big, he said, admiring the ass he was fucking as cum leaked from her dilated asshole.

What about underwear?She asked, reminding him why he was able to do this.

Well, it's not waterproof, he said, seeing the soaked fabric hanging loosely on his lucky body.

So I did a good job? You learned something new.

RUN!

Extraordinary work.

RUN!

Oh man, she moaned and groaned.

RUN!

Finish your shower, get dressed and I'll take you home.

RUN!

Finally, damn it, he sighed in relief.

RUN! Oh, she screamed, probably thinking he was done spanking her huge ass, but instead she wanted to spank him some more. It was so big.

Jeff got out of the shower, dried himself with several towels, and wasted them jerking off to the social media profiles of hot, young, curvy women. But now her only obsession was her nudity, her pleasure and the cum flowing from her asshole. Now he had a real deal and she was contractually obligated to move on.

Chapter 8

Jeff smiled from ear to ear as he got dressed and gave the poor girl a well-deserved spank.

The way to her was quiet, she said nothing, she sat there with a grimace, with her arms crossed and her beautiful legs.

Jeff should have felt bad, but he didn't feel bad about it. To be honest, he just wanted more, so he demanded more. Rhonda said nothing as his hands ran up and down her thighs, touching them upwards and squeezing the huge muscles.

Can you stop? – she asked him while he felt her legs crossed for a good ten minutes.

I can't do that, he admitted.

I don't wear underwear. I have no contractual obligation to allow you to use my body.

Then why do I let you touch me? » he asked her, still holding her hand as he guided her, trying to slip between her shapely thighs and feel her naked pussy under her miniskirt.

Just... drive me home.

Are you sure that's where you want to go?Back with her boyfriend?

If you take me back to my family, Dad will see me beaming after what you did, find your address and kill you. But my friend won't notice...

- But why?

I am not with him because of his mind.

He's not even with you in spirit, said Jeff, laughing.

I told you to stop touching me! She tried to pull her hand away, but he just slapped her on the thigh.

I know, I'm so hard, he said, flexing his powerful quadriceps muscles.

That's not my problem.

You are the cause.

Then continue.

I can't, not with you here, he said and slowed the car to the bus stop.

Then I'll take the subway home, he said and grabbed the handle.

Jeff closed the door and she turned around with her mouth open.

Open it.

And some idiot raped you while you were walking down the street? No, I care about you too much to let that happen.

I won't let myself be raped and you don't care about me. Just my body.

That's not true, I like you too. It's just that your body...

Open the door.

Dressed like that?You look sluttier than the sluts who serve on the streets, and it's well past midnight. You will definitely be raped if I let you go. Women are not made like you. No vile person can resist the fact that you are gone.

He sighed and crossed his arms.

I'm right, aren't I?

Okay, he gave in. What should I do?

I want you to fix the problem you caused and forget about me touching you.

Now?

All the way back, he insisted.

You're a fucking pig, you know that?

I've known that for a long time. Now crawl towards me, Rhonda.

Rhonda had already removed her belt, she just had to stop herself from crawling towards him like the whore he knew she was, but this change of heart. He knew what the dirty side of her angelic and perfect beauty wanted now and what was evil. She crawled over to him and lay on her stomach, and he was happy to change gears on his fancy steering wheel. She was an expert at pulling out his cock and her small, manicured hand couldn't even grip the strap. By the way, you don't cover my face or my body. My boyfriend can't see me with cum.

So there is only one option-

Can I cum in your shoes? It's an automatic car, right? You only need one foot.

If that's the deal, I'm not going anywhere.

When Jeff felt the slut's complete submission, he grunted and pulled her onto his cock. Colera! You're so good at sucking cock! He moaned a moment later as Rhonda's tongue expertly wrapped around his cock and she pushed his entire shaft back into her mouth. Oh damn! When I first saw those plump lips, I knew you would be the best cocksucker! Cholera! Jeff groaned through gritted teeth as Rhonda blew harder on him.

Mmmmmmm, do you like fucking my mouth on your big cock while my boyfriend is waiting for me at home? – Rhonda asked in a sexual manner, taking her mouth off his cock for a moment before greedily devouring it again .

Fuck! Jeff cried out in pleasure. You're fucking good at this! Damn, you were born to suck cock, damn it! He half growled, half teased and Rhonda purred as she allowed him to fill her mouth with cock. Her lips immediately wrapped around the thick shaft and her tongue began cutting and moving wildly as she sucked hard and fast. Her mouth twisted as she took his cock between her lips and sent it back down her throat as she sucked harder and harder. Rhonda was determined to give Jeff the best blowjob she had ever given. It was like she was desperate to suck the cum out of his balls and recklessly filled her mouth with his hard cock.

The whole car was filled with the illicit sound of a hot blowjob as Rhonda's platinum blonde hair, no longer straight after everything Jeff had given her, swayed back and forth in curly waves that cascaded down her back as he fucked her up and down. the impressive shaft of a handsome man.

Mmmmm, your cock is so big! I love it! Rhonda purred, taking her mouth off his cock to catch her breath. Jeff smiled dazedly at him, his chest rising and falling with heavy breathing.

Damn, it did him good! He could barely keep his eyes on the road.

Do you like seeing your cock in my mouth? Rhonda joked, turning to him to enjoy his intense gaze. The sunglasses obscured the stars in his eyes as Jeff's beauty made her swoon.

Shit.... You're so damn awesome! Jeff answered honestly, running his hand over her flat stomach, enjoying the feel of her taut muscles and the gold piercing in her sexy belly button.

And you are the worst, biggest, most disgusting pig I have ever seen. Rhonda giggled before turning around, her huge ass returning as she lay perfectly on her side and her mouth quickly found his cock

And yet I'm the best fuck you've ever had, he declared and she

pushed him away with one hand without helping him with the

blowjob.

Chapter 9

Rhonda moved her head up and down quickly so that her wavy hair bounced in time with her shaking breasts, and sucked hard and fast. Jeff's thick cockhead hit her tight throat repeatedly as his lips met her fist, moving up and down and swirling his tongue.

When Jeff saw that huge ass, completely naked, those firm, round cheeks in such a perfect pose, he raised his hand.

RUN!

Mmmmm, I love it when you spank me, Rhonda moaned as she tried to catch her breath. Do you want to cum for me, Jeff? Rhonda purred as she breathed, brushing her long hair out of her face before sliding back down his shaft.

Shit! If you suck me like that, I'll puke down your throat! Jeff cried out loudly, his chest rising and falling as he tried to hold back the best sucking he had ever experienced. When he said that, Rhonda gasped and a shiver ran through her. Fuck, I want you to cum in my mouth, Jeff! I want you to use me like a whore! Rhonda replied absentmindedly before turning back to his huge cock. The blonde sucked like a wild whore, giving it her all and fucking wildly as Jeff moaned and groaned while Rhonda panted through her nose and sucked hungrily.

She really wanted him to come. I want to taste it and swallow every drop. She's hungry for cum and just the thought of her boyfriend waiting at home while she has her mouth full of her boss' cock excites her so much that her juices start flowing.

Jeff witnessed the warmest and most wonderful sight he had ever seen. The incredibly greasy snack on his lap, so strange and beautiful at the same time.

Damn! But it was incredible! His lips were smooth, warm and wet at the same time. Damn, those sexy lips were stretched suggestively into an O as she fought to take every inch of him into her mouth, hitting the back of his throat with each thrust deep into her lewd opening.

Damn, she was beautiful! The sight of her beautiful face wrapped around his cock was almost enough to make Jeff cum. And come strong. He was already so close after she had sucked his cock for so long that he knew he couldn't last much longer because he had never experienced a blowjob this good. That shocked him.

I don't mind being your whore, but if I'm going to be, I better do a little more, Rhonda said as she caught her breath and his hand found her clit.

OH? Jeff asked with a raised eyebrow, watching in amusement as she became aroused just by sucking his cock, and the more he touched her clit, digging his fingers in and feeling her G-spot, the more she squirmed on his lap.

Mhm. Rhonda meowed, her toes curling in pleasure. Get ready to cum down your whore's throat, Jeff. Rhonda laughed, then he did something he wasn't expecting and damn, his balls almost burst! Rhonda sucked hard and ran her mouth up and down his cock repeatedly, licking and coating his shaft with even more saliva than before. And then as she closed her mouth one last time and the head of his cock sank deep into her throat, she paused and slowly...oh so slowly... he pushed his cock deep into her throat.

The slut worked harder and harder, determined to slit his throat, and it almost scared him how little attention she paid to her boyfriend, but she was the hottest slut he'd ever met, the way she drove her cock pushed into the narrowness of his throat.

Jeff nearly lost his all bearings! The feel of her tight, wet throat wrapping around his dick was so intense. Holy fuck, whore. Keep taking more.

Jeff's hand left her climaxing pussy, his work on her g-spot complete as she was gushing with juices while gagging on his cock. He reached out and placed his hand on her crop top and cupped her huge breast.

Rhonda was on fire as her orgasm rocked her world, his skilled fingers manipulating her in all the right ways as she pleasured his cock religiously. At first she just stood still, gagging and coughing, then very slowly and deliberately she pulled the big head away and let his cock slip almost out of her mouth, then she quickly slid her mouth down the roaring rod to the thick tip. it was forced down his throat again. Once, twice, three times, four times Rhonda repeated this pattern until she could easily, even carefully, take the head of his cock into her throat, then she slowly began to gain weight again. Finally she fucked his cock just as fast and hard as before, but this time she stuck it an inch deep into her throat.The sounds of his gagging and sucking joined his moans as they filled the Mustang illicitly, but Rhonda didn't care, she just fucked his mouth wildly. And Jeff... he had to do everything he could to resist and not come, son!

Mmmmm, I love your cock! Rhonda purred as she pulled his cock out of her mouth for a moment, gasping for air, before she collapsed onto his cock and hungrily swallowed six inches of it. It's probably the same as your mouth and throat! Damned!!If you keep sucking my cock, I'll cum! Jeff moaned loudly and massaged her breasts as he drove towards south London. Shit, but Jeff could barely contain himself as her whole body began to shake from the twisting of her stiff nipples and those sexy thighs rubbing together as the slut basked in the pleasure.

Curse this bitch was destined to please men. Her entire fucking body, built to be pleasured the way the sensations spread all the way down to her toes as they curled and twitched in those gorgeous heels.

Over and over, she bobbed her head furiously, sucking and slurping, slobbering and sucking, as she gagged and swallowed more and more. Until finally, Rhonda slowed once again and eased another inch down her throat! Rhonda stood perfectly straight and played with her big tits in his huge hand. She buried the extra inch in her throat much faster than the first inch. But she took her time with the first few juices before she started slapping his face up and down again.

Once Jeff had regained control of himself, Rhonda stopped again and took another, then another, and the last inch of his cock down her throat until she was gagging, her heart pounding, her mouth covering the base of his cock, hers Finger played with his balls as she gagged and coughed.

Fuck! Jeff exhaled and squeezed her stiff nipples so hard that she screamed and her mouth and throat were full of cock. She shook her head like crazy, fast and hard, over and over again, fucking her mouth on his cock like her life depended on it.

Shit! SHIT! Was all Jeff could sing at first as waves of intense pleasure washed over his body, almost making him weak in the knees.

MMMMMPHHHH!Rhonda moaned around his cock, fucking wildly up and down the thick shaft that smelled like cheese.

Exactly, bitch! FUCK! Ugh! Fuck your tight throat on my cock! Phew! Suck my cock like your life depends on it! » Jeff groaned, digging his fingers into her firm breasts.

The feeling in his hand was like a hammer hitting the cum in your balls. At this point he almost exploded in her mouth as she almost repeatedly removed her mouth from his cock before slamming it shut. Her breasts were deliciously soft, but so hard that his cock throbbed in her throat at the touch. And he held her tits by the waist while the slut continued to furiously fuck her mouth with his cock.

Shit, Rhonda, what the fuck, right? By God, it's beautiful! He cried out and squeezed her breasts tightly in his hands.

Rhonda responded with a loud moan, arching her back again and groping her breast into his hand. And boy, did Jeff put it to good use. Press and massage firmly.

Take my cock, bitch! Bitch! Suck my cock, you wonderful fuck toy! Jeff exclaimed, his mind whirling about her sucking his cock.

. Rhonda's mouth touched the base of Jeff's cock again and again as she took every inch he could give her. With every fold of her lips, Rhonda's roommate became faster and more efficient at sucking his entire cock. He takes fewer breaks and lowers his head less often.

The blonde beauty bobbed her head up and down, fucking her tight throat like crazy. She moans and pants around her mouth full of cock as Jeff moans in pure ecstasy!

The pleasure overwhelms him until he thinks he might pass out! Damn, she was good at that! He pulled out his soaking wet cock and ran it over every inch of him until he felt dizzy and could barely breathe.

Damn! Damn, she was the best cocksucker he had ever met!

As his whole world began to spin and happiness flowed through every vein in his body, Jeff suddenly couldn't hold back anymore. Grabbing the beauty's head, he quickly tightened his grip and held her in place, his cock immediately filling her mouth after exiting her throat again. He pushed his hips forward, slid his cock down the slut's throat, held her tight and began thrusting his cock in and out of the slut's mouth and down her throat as hard as he could while feeling as he came closer.

The wet sounds of Jeff's cock pumping between her soft lips echoed throughout the car and were met with the blonde gagging every time Jeff pushed his cock down her throat. He fucked her mouth and throat again and again, fucking her face wildly, and she could only endure it as his tongue twitched wildly.

The sight of her on her knees, calmly taking his cock down her throat and filling her mouth as she watched her tits move and shake obscenely with each thrust was too much for Jeff, and after he took her in After being face fucked hard for a few minutes, he roughly let go of her hair and gasped for air.

As we slowed the car down a dark alley, the headlights spotted a dead end ahead, bags of trash strewn across the Dickson walls of closed stores, and a large puddle of water between the car and the dead end.

Rhonda didn't miss a beat, as her hands left his head, she slammed her face into the floor and swallowed his entire cock again. She angrily shoved her face up and down his cock, pushing him deep into her tight throat, over and over, faster and harder, sucking furiously on his cock as if she would die if he stopped. Rhonda loved his huge cock like a woman possessed. Desperate to make him cum, Rhonda flicked her tongue and danced wildly, sucking his cock harder than ever before. And the pleasure was too much for Jeff as he stiffened. His balls were moving, ready to explode down the whore's throat.

Ugh, damn! Take that cock, Rhonda! Jeff moaned, his eyes almost rolling in pleasure as her warm, wet mouth brought him pleasure.

She sucked like crazy, up and down, over and over, taking the cock ten inches deep into her throat. Over and over and over again. I fucked her tight throat like the slut she was. And then Jeff's thrusts on her descending lips suddenly became erratic. Her hands grabbed his hair again.Fight, fight, fight!

MMmmmmmmph!Mmmmph! Mmmmmmmph! Rhonda moaned; her throat full of cock. His tongue moved wildly as his mouth moved up and down.

Oh shit, Rhonda! Female dog! You are awesome! Female dog! You will make me cum! » said Jeff, his voice tense and full of joy. He redoubled his efforts, sucking as hard and as fast as he could. Her head was dazed and in the car you could hear the sound of her wet, well-fucked mouth gently hitting the base of Jeff's cock.

Suddenly Jeff stiffened and his whole body tensed. He slammed her head against the base of his cock, her nose digging into his balls as he held her there.

AAAAGGGHHHHHH! FFFUUUCCK! I'm about to cum, you fucking whore! Crap! WHORE! YES! I'm coming, bitch! Shit, I'm cumming in your strange mouth! Jeff suddenly screamed and put more pressure on his head, the air being forced from his lungs as his testicles blooked his nose and made it impossible for him to breathe.

Rhonda stood still, panting, just in pleasure as the thick cock expanded in her throat.

Rhonda barely had time to moan before a huge rope of thick, sticky white cum shot from Jeff's cock down her throat. Another big ball followed, then another as the big bastard started giving her his cum. As the thicker mucus flowed down her throat, Rhonda swallowed quickly and felt the thick mucus flow down her throat and into her stomach.

Jeff choked on his cock and pinched her balls. He felt like he was dying and let her breathe as he came again and again, pouring a stream of cum down her throat. He breathed through his nose, staying at the base and squirting cum into her.

He swallowed loudly. A thick stream of Jeff's cum ran down her throat as she swallowed, but more came until drops escaped from the corner of her mouth around his cock and ran down her chin. Jeff came endlessly, pounding her throat and filling her mouth with his powerful seed until Rhonda could barely stop swallowing. He felt his stomach fill and his eyes widened in shock as he saw how much Jeff was actually about to cum! She even felt cum coming out of her nose as she tried to breathe, but it wasn't working properly as it flooded her with gallons of cum.

RUN! Rhonda managed to drink everything and smelled what came to her nose.

RUN!

Rhonda looked up and saw her phone glowing and vibrating in the cradle on the dashboard. Her boyfriend's name and photo on the screen.

RUN!

I think you'll have to answer him soon, said Jeff, squeezing his round cheeks. – Unless you don't want to?

RUN!

I don't know, he said.

RUN!

At least you have to cover your ass. I left a mark there.

SLAP!

I've never been beaten up so often.I coo your hands!

SLAP!

I know.

RUN!

Rhonda took off her miniskirt, sat on the seat and fed herself the ropes of cum hanging out of her nose.Will it be the same tomorrow?

Jeff smiled at him. When you run into the office tomorrow, wear something sexy.

You only do that to me when I'm wear

I just fucked your throat, he reminded her.

And you're a bastard for doing this.

But did you like it?

Did I say no?

Maybe you'd like me to take your sweaty body into the shower tomorrow morning when you get back to work?Maybe kick his ass?

Don't try!

I think you would like that, wouldn't you? I have to go, she said, but she stayed where she was and he reached out to caress her large breasts.

Then go away.Your friend is waiting for you. He is there and calling you.

If I wear what I normally wear for running, can you promise to leave me alone?

Should I do it? Churches.

Where the hell are we? He looked around and the car lights illuminated several needles scattered among the bags. You didn't answer my question, slut, he said, placing his hand on her thigh. What do you want? – he asked, knowing exactly where he had taken her.In a remote part of South London where the alleys were dark, eerie and always quiet.

That was the ultimate goal of the old office whores. However, he usually brought them here when he was sure they were ready to meet her. But he had never had a slut so young, so big, so beautiful and so sensual that he could push her to her limits.

From the first damn day he thought she was ready for the final fuck.Rhonda's eyes quickly glanced at his still erect penis and then quickly looked outwards.

Jeff looked at the puddle and felt his blood boil as he remembered the thick, medium, thin waste he had spread between the baskets. Their screams, echoing off the surrounding gray Dickson walls, drowned out the hops. He unbuckled the car's seatbelt, turned on the dashboard camera, and exited the moving vehicle so the camera's lights could help capture details.

Time passed so slowly as he put his cock in his pants and walked around the car.She watched him walk toward her while she was texting and hastily put her phone away until he stopped at the window and opened the door. Come out, slut, he ordered, looking at her and she bit her lip.

It rains a lot, he said hesitantly.

I don't care. Now go, he said as he ran his black hand through her hair, grabbing the blonde locks and pulling as she let him decide.

Oh shit, she cried as he pulled her out of the car and pushed her forward. What are you doing?She asked as she fell, her heels crunching beneath her as she fell to her knees.

I'm going to break you, he said as he placed his boot on her back, causing her stomach to fall into a puddle. Rhonda groaned and froze as he grabbed her by the hips and lifted her so that she lay in the puddle with her arms beside her, rubbing against the black garbage bags. Her knees were pressed to the floor and part of her face was pressed to the floor while her skirt fell in a bunch down her back and her bare bottom was in the spotlight.

Her cheeks were so round and wide that the space created was a good slide for rainwater, which soaked her miniskirt and crop top as she lay there and she felt him playing with her belt buckle. Rhonda panicked but remained paralyzed as she waited. Literally caught in the spotlight until his belt hit her from behind.

SWAT!

Ahhhh! She screamed.

SWAT!

Oh man! – he screamed as his fat ass was hit again.

SWAT!

I'm not wearing it...Underwear – tried to remind herself and him what they were missing and that they couldn't do it.

Jeff ripped off her soaking wet miniskirt and did the same to her crop top. Throwing soaked clothes into garbage bags, which stank and some of the juice dripped into a puddle.

Ugh, she moaned as he fastened the belt around her neck.

RUN!

You're my whore, Rhonda, he said, running his hands over her big, bare cheeks, and I don't care about our contract anymore.

RUN!Rhonda tensed and held her breath as she felt the tip of his cock touch her impressive anus. But-

RUN! No more excuses, she said, placing her hands on either side of her head. The tall man loomed over her as the tip of the mushroom pressed against her sphincter.

It's still so big, she moans as the black cock slides into her. Why are you still so tall?

A lot of Viagra, stamina and experience, he said, placing a huge hand onto her head, pushing her face further into the puddle. All in preparation for you, but I didn't think we'd get here today. I thought we would use weeks breaking you in, but you're like me, Rhonda. You crave this, need this, and have an endless appetite for it. So, to hell with the excuses, the technicalities and the pretence that you give a damn about the boyfriend you probably texted a lie to before I pulled you from the car.To hell with all of this. You can't stop me from hurting you, bitch. That's you, Oliwia. A curvy beauty, a fat little Latina with an ass so big you forget she has big tits too. The perfect little toy to fuck with...on the street ! He groaned and pushed his big black cock deep into her ass, her big butt cheeks slapping and bouncing as he slapped and lifted her ass, her back arching as he entered her.. on the streets of London. In a dark alley, in a puddle, next to smelly garbage bags and used needles...He pounded her big ass with his big black cock. His stomach slapped against his round cheeks, hitting them with every downward thrust. He fucks her so hard that her big tits fall into a puddle with every thrust.

AHHHHH! FUCK!Rhonda screamed into the puddle, on her knees, ass in the air, tits pressed into the dirty water, hands at her sides as he began destroying her ass.

Oof! Fuck you! Jeff moaned, no longer holding back.His hand using her head as support as he lifted himself up and let his fat belly weigh him down and give the thrusts so much force she whaled like a siren.

AAAAAAAHHHHHHHH! she screamed into the puddle, her clapping ass cheeks music to his ears as the sticky juices previously left behind in her connected their crotches like spider webs.

The asshole was wide now, taking him deeper and the cum he had left behind in it previously lay itself around his shaft as he demolished her big ass.

AAAAAHHHHHHHHH!– she screamed as the rain pelted her face.

Damn, this ass is made for black cocks, right? I've never had a slut with such a big ass who could take my cock like you and hear the slap of those big cheeks. ..Daddy can't get enough of you.

WHAT! DAMNED! Beat my ass, daddy! AHHHH! Rhonda squirted, now completely consenting as he hit her.

Dad always shared the office whores with his employees, but I don't want to share this ass. They wouldn't know what to do with that thickness. Man, this is incredible, he marveled at the huge ass he had smashed.

Ah! Keep fucking me, daddy!AAHHH! » he groaned and squeezed his buttocks with pleasure. around him. You want me all to yourself, don't you? It's going to be hard, Dad!But I'll try to resist him! As long as you fuck me...

CLICKS! His face contorted from the impact and he tightened his belt. Gagging her and fucking her hard in the ass are the same thing.

CLICKS!

As long as I do what the fuck?

CLICKS!

As long as you fuck me-

CLICKS!

I like…

CLICKS!

That!

CLICKS! Jeff could no longer hold this position, his strong arms growing tired as he straightened himself up, his cock retreating to the entrance of her anus before he grabbed her by the hips, leaning down and continuing to slap her bruised cheeks.

RUN!

I can't believe how hard you fucked me, daddy!Uh! And you always go! Damn it, daddy! Give me your black cock! Straight into my ass!Give me more! she screamed for more. Pleasure trembled through her body, her ass cheeks jiggling so seductively as she continued with wild thrusts.

RUN!

You're not going home to your boyfriend tonight, he said, grabbing the belt and pulling her back, choking her hard and lifting her upper body as he fucked her back and forth in the puddle water.She ruined her curvy body as she took it screaming.

AAAAAAAAAAAAAAA!!!!!

TATODDDDDDDDDDDDDDDDDDDDDDDDDDDDDDDDDDDDD DDDDDDDDDDDDDDDDDDDDDDDDDDDDDDDDDDDDDDDDD DDDDDDDDDDDDDD

KLAS!

RUN!

And damn, you get it in all your dirty holes!

RUN!

I WANT IT! PLEASE!I NEED IT! she begged for his dominance between her moans.

RUN!

If you want to keep this up, slut, he said, tugging on her waist like a rag doll, then you'll find a way to make each fuck better than the last and show me how much you want this black guy. cock to keep stuffing you.

RUN!

I want it, daddy! I want more! ALL THE FUCKING TIME!

RUN!

Do you want to come with me, bitch?From that black cock pounding your ass? Jeff asked, feeling the pressure building in his balls.

RUN!

Ugh! I'm close!Rhonda gasped and could barely contain herself as her body began to tremble.

RUN!

YUMI Jeff ordered, not slowing down, not slowing down as he penetrated her deep and hard.

RUN!

Ugh! GOD! Rhonda moaned, her body shaking, her ass slapping, and her tongue hanging out, limping like the rest of her as she followed his commands.

RUN!

Chapter 10

Jeff grabbed a handful of her long, straight hair, pushed it back tightly, and lifted the top half out of the puddle. Then he upped the ante by fucking her with longer, deeper and more powerful thrusts. He slowed his pace slightly as he tried to gain access to the deepest part of her ass.

RUN!

AHHHHHHH!WHORE! WHORE! WHORE! OHHHHHHH! she moaned, her body shaking with unbridled pleasure, taking her to the gates of hell and beyond, into the endless abyss of filth.

Do it, damn it! Just do it! Come back! - He ordered her, without slowing down, to hit her hard.

Oof! Tel! Tel! HURRY! HURRY! HURRY! FUCK! Rhonda moaned, her body trembling, a strong tug on her hair supporting her upper half as her black master continued to drill her hard, her entire body trembling and her breasts swaying lewdly beneath her. GOD! Phew! WHORE! WHORE! OHHHHH! he groaned.

UGGGGH! Jeff groaned, closing one eye and trying to hold back the impending pleasure. His entire naked body was tense, his muscles tense and working together to keep from shattering his brain and stopping the flow of cum pooling in his balls.

I'm getting closer!

Me too, Dad! I plan on coming back! Don't stop hitting me! she screamed, her juices squirting all over his cock and her body shaking beneath him.

I'm going to cum inside you! He moaned as he continued to fuck her, unable to stop drilling her asshole, and no matter how many times he saw her round cheeks jiggle with his thrusts, it was an encouragement, it to continue doing.

Give me your cum! She screamed and moaned as he dominated her ass.OHHHHH! Rhonda screamed and her pussy gushed again.

Finally the waves of pleasure left her, leaving her exhausted body completely at his mercy. He continued to drill, releasing her hair to grab her raised hips again and unleashing all his energy to destroy her ass.

SPANK!

CUM IN ME!! she screamed.

Fuck it, he said and pulled out of her ass.

What are you-

RUN!

Jeff pushed his cock into her pussy. I will raise you.

RUN!

OH FUCK, EEEEEESS!BREEEEEEEEEEEE! »

RUN!

Ugh! Crap! It happens! He groaned as he rounded the corner, almost seething as he slapped his large cheeks left and right.

RUN!

Shit! Crap! Crap! Jeff moaned and moved his hips.

RUN!

Wow! Jeff groaned, his hips acting on pure instinct, burying the entire length of his big hard cock, all the way down to the balls, into her hungry pussy just as the first rocket of cum poured out of him.

RUN!

AHHHHHHHHHHHHHHHH! Rhonda screamed, clenching her pussy and welcoming the straining cock, releasing a torrent of accumulated cum.

Fuck! Jeff grunted and shot his sperm into the slut's womb, her perfect pussy gushing out of him as he pumped deep into the barely eighteen year old girl's fertile, unprotected pussy.

OOOOOHHHHH CHHHIIITTTT!Rhonda screamed, the feeling of all that cum filling her was driving her crazy. Her walls milked the cum out of him, squeezing and gripping his pumping cock as he continued pounding her big ass.

Jeff continued to fuck, drive and thrust his big cock into her, filling her and pumping his sperm into her fertile womb. He fell and caught himself after slipping out of her pussy. The black cock rested between her round cheeks as the last jets of cum squirted from her sex and hit the sides of her face and back.Neither passed out, but both were recovering from the most intense sex they had ever participated in, left breathless and struggling to find the strength to move. Her body wrapped around his and stayed on top. His legs gave out as they fell to the side and his arms lost all strength and fell to the bed. He finally found the strength to stand up and look at his naked, sweaty whore.

KILLING!

Who are you?

RUN!

Oh man…. I'm your bitch, daddy.

RUN!

Show your commitment, slut, and jerk off for me.

RUN!

As you wish, Daddy, she moaned, standing naked, full of cum flowing to her unprotected balls, her back and face covered in cum as she twisted her big ass and made her slapping cheeks shake .

RUN! Bastard, he sighed, unable to move his body. She was ready and really liked that position, head in the air and face down. He felt comfortable and the cold English rain pleasantly soothed his bruised cheeks. You fucked me so good, she moaned and purred, shaking her big ass against her black daddy.

Jeff grabbed his ass and stroked the huge muscles.

RUN!

Oh, I need more, Daddy, she begged insatiably as his black cock pounded into her. Put it in me already, he moaned, insatiable for the black cock.

RUN!

Fuck, I really turned you on, Jeff said, shoving his softening cock into her cum-filled pussy.

RUN!

Oh my God! he grimaced and groaned.

RUN!

The best ass I've ever seen!

RUN!

Oh man! It's all yours, Dad!She screamed and felt his stupid, violent thrusts.

RUN!

Good girl, he said, slapping her big ass as he destroyed her.

RUN!

Oh, that hurt!

RUN!

I know, but your ass can take a lot more.

RUN!

We still have time before we have to leave this place.

RUN!

But my body…

RUN!

That's what it's made for and after a night in bed...Let's start putting some more power in your ass because next time I want to fuck you really good, he said with a laugh.

RUN!

Oh come on, you evil bastard! – she growled, tired of the teasing. Then fuck my ass properly!

RUN!

Holy shit, he said, enjoying her body, we're going to have so much fun with you. Not even one damn challenge will break you.

RUN!

Oh man! She moaned and moaned and moaned, her body just reacting to the pleasure and dirt as he used her and broke her even more.

RUN!

Did you ever grow up like that, bitch? Jeff asked, making her applaud.

RUN!

Never, he sighed and groaned.

RUN!

We both knew this was going to happen the first time you put that big ass on my lap, he said, grabbing her hips and fucking her so hard that her big ass cheeks slapped and slapped her in the small of her back .

It was merciless.

RUN!

You did it on purpose, didn't you? You tortured me and showed me what I wanted. You dared me to do this to you. You may not have thought about it, but your body was trying to tell you. Admit it. I wanted it from the start!

RUN!

OH YES! I wanted your black cock from the first time!!!She screamed and swayed as her juices leaked from her cum filled pussy.

RUN!

Tell me that you want my children! Say it and come! »

RUN!

I want your children! – he screamed, shaking and trembling with orgasm.

RUN!

Damn, what a bitch I unlocked, right? Man, think if cumming in your pussy will make you fall...

RUN!

I wouldn't mind having a little pregnancy fat on me, he said, running his hands over her juicy ass. Make it even bigger! He laughs. If that's possible! Damn, that ass is big!

RUN!

Are you the one who wants to talk? You and your big black cock pushing me in, filling me, using me...interrupt me. Oh, it's so big, she moaned, her mind racing with desire, pleasure and pain. I want you to fuck me harder than you've ever fucked anyone else, Daddy! I want every inch of your big black cock to explode with cum in my fucking belly! See if you're man enough to pour it!

RUN!

Damn, you were born for this, weren't you? Barely legal and built like that? You will lose a lot of money if you don't do porn.

RUN!

Oh man, you're ruining me! Oh shit! You're right! My body is built for dirt...

RUN!

And who gets to enjoy your dirty, sexy body, slut?

RUN!

Oh, my ugly, fat, black daddy! You have my ass!

RUN!

Fuck, admit it, you're going to be my fuck toy, slut!

RUN!

Hit your toy, daddy!

RUN!

Have you ever imagined going in and fucking on the edge of a garbage can? Have you ever wondered how unkempt you would be?

RUN!

Oh man! I never thought I would fall so low! But I love this!

RUN!

And what does that make you, bitch?

RUN!

BLACK COCK FUCK!

RUN!

What a disgusting bitch you are, Rhonda.

RUN!

The best, he said jokingly. Now come inside your slut and fuck me, daddy!

RUN!

9 7 9 8 8 9 0 3 6 1 0 0 4